HOCKEY SUPER SIX

HAT TRICKED

BY KEVIN SYLVESTER

Scholastic Canada Ltd.
Toronto New York London Auckland Sydney
Mexico City New Delhi Hong Kong Buenos Aires

Dedicated 2 Gretzky #99, Perreault #11, Sauve #31, Briere #48 and Howe #9!

Scholastic Canada Ltd.
604 King Street West, Toronto, Ontario M5V 1E1, Canada

Scholastic Inc.
557 Broadway, New York, NY 10012, USA

Scholastic Australia Pty Limited
PO Box 579, Gosford, NSW 2250, Australia

Scholastic New Zealand Limited
Private Bag 94407, Botany, Manukau 2163, New Zealand

Scholastic Children's Books
Euston House, 24 Eversholt Street, London NW1 1DB, UK

www.scholastic.ca

Library and Archives Canada Cataloguing in Publication
Title: Hat tricked / Kevin Sylvester.
Names: Sylvester, Kevin, author, illustrator.
Series: Sylvester, Kevin. Hockey super six.
Description: Series statement: Hockey super six
Identifiers: Canadiana (print) 20210154039 | Canadiana (ebook) 20210154063 |
ISBN 9781443182935 (softcover) | ISBN 9781443191739 (ebook)
Classification: LCC PS8637.Y42 H38 2021 | DDC C813/.6—dc23

6 5 4 3 2 1   Printed in Canada 114   21 22 23 24 25

MIX
Paper from
responsible sources
FSC® C016245

SECURITY CLEARANCE: RED LEVEL THREE

Only the most **DEDICATED** (hint, hint) can figure out the `SIX-FIGURE PASSCODE` to access this latest adventure of the Hockey Super Six.*

NICE WORK, CODE-BREAKER.

But before you enter the third — **AND MOST PERILOUS** — mission of the Hockey Super Six, a **WARNING.*** Have some tissues ready to wipe away those tears.

And you will need repeated warnings. Because, you see, this is a sad book. **VERY** sad. **SUPER** sad.

NOW, first: A RECAP of the adventures of the Super Six so far!

---

*For all of you who snuck this book into school, this warning will pop up each time you should get ready for a good cry.

If you see this 🤧 grab a tissue, or stop reading before you turn into a sobbing mess on your classroom floor. That's SURE to get you in hot water (and this story requires FROZEN water).

IN OUR PREVIOUS ADVENTURE

SIX HOCKEY-LOVING GEEKS WERE...

WHO ARE YOU CALLING A GEEK?

YEAH... THEY'RE GEEKS.

...ZAPPED BY A MYSTERIOUS FREEZE RAY...

...FIRED BY THIS DUDE, CLARENCE CROSSCHECK.

I'M THE BADDEST GUY!

WITH THE EVILIEST IDEAS!

Their new mission? **TO FIND AND CAPTURE ONE FURRY BUNNY RABBIT. THIS RABBIT.** Look how **CUTE** he is!

What could possibly go wrong with such a simple mission?

Oh . . . **SO. VERY. VERY. MUCH.**

Tissues ready?

But first . . . a comic book tutorial on **CONTEXT** and **PERSPECTIVE**!

SAME BUNNY, BUT IN CONTEXT YOU NOW SEE ITS TRUE SIZE.

THIS CHANGES MY PERSPECTIVE OF THINGS... INCLUDING MY PERSONAL SAFETY.

SEE? CONTEXT!

SO, GIVING YOU THE PROPER CONTEXT, YOU CAN NOW PERCEIVE OR SEE HOW DANGEROUS THIS MISSION WILL ACTUALLY TURN OUT TO BE.

BUNNY SMASH!

!?

VERY DANGEROUS. ≋UHNNNNNNNN≋

CHAPTER ONE
FUR-OCIOUS

The Super Six sat on the benches of their locker room, sweating and smiling.

"Good practice," Karl, the team's captain, said.

"I only gave up one goal," DJ said.

"BUT WE BOTH SCORED!" said the twins, Benny and Jenny.

"Maybe, but I can barely tell you apart, so I only count it as one goal," DJ said with a shrug.

Starlight and Mo exchanged a glance. They were the defence pair on the team and had only allowed the twins a handful of shots total. Mo was about to lecture DJ on the nature of "teamwork" when Ron Dell, the (former Crosscheck minion, now friendly) robot ran into the room.

"**URGENT MESSAGE, TEAM,**" Ron said. He pushed a button on his butt. A woman stood in a thin beam of light coming out of his eye.

"Help me, Obi-Wan."

"Oops," said Ron. "Let's try that again." He pushed his butt twice and the woman was replaced by a **FLICKERING IMAGE OF A CUTE BUNNY RABBIT.** "This is Mr. Fuzzywinkle ... BEFORE THE EXPERIMENTS."

Mr. Fuzzywinkle sat inside a magician's top hat, quietly nibbling on a carrot.

"He was part of the

ice skating show *Blades of Magic*. El Slapo would place an empty hat at centre ice and Mr. Fuzzywinkle would appear inside, as if out of thin air. Crosscheck discovered the bunny was digging a hole under the hat, and trapped him. Then he did this—"

The image vibrated as the gloved hand of **Clarence Crosscheck** — evil goalie/scientist — appeared and tied a **SMALL BLACK STRAP**, like a wristband, around the bunny's leg.

"THAT'S THE SAME KIND OF WRISTBAND CROSSCHECK USED TO MAKE KARL EVEN GOOFIER!" said the twins.

The others chuckled, except Karl of course, until they saw what the wristband did to cute little Mr. Fuzzywinkle. His eyes bugged out.

He twitched like he'd been zapped, and shook like a leaf in a hurricane. Then he stopped. He lifted his head, revealing **EYES RED WITH RAGE**.

There was a blood-curdling growl as the bunny lunged at Ron, who screamed as the image dissolved into static.

"This was when Crosscheck was first experimenting with mind control. Using animals." Ron shuddered. "I feel so guilty about all this."

Mo placed a hand on Ron's round head. "You're a good guy now, Ron."

"Thanks," Ron sniffed. "I took off the wristband, but the **DAMAGE WAS DONE**."

"Poor little fella," DJ said. He was always warning the others about dangerous animals — like nuclear chickens and ice-loving sharks. But seeing one "created" right in front of his eyes shook him. As a goalie, he felt an affinity with the weirdos of the world, radioactive rabbits included.

Ron sighed. "Crosscheck, of course, wanted more. He zapped Mr. Fuzzywinkle with the **SIZEMATRON 2000**. That just made him **BIGGER AND EVEN MEANER.**"*

Ron turned off the image. "Mr. Fuzzywinkle also showed an almost magical ability to disappear and reappear, causing lots of damage. You remember the sinkholes that swallowed up all those houses in Florida?"

"That was the bunny?" DJ asked.

Ron nodded. "Crosscheck was fine with it, until Fuzzy dumped his time-share laboratory in

---

*If you were paying attention in the earlier books, you'll remember from the Squids that "getting even meaner" is a side effect of Crosscheck's SIZEMATRON 2000 ray gun.

a lagoon. So we caught him and locked him in a high-security cage."

"Until he escaped that too," Starlight said.

"**A REAL HARRY HOUDINI**," said Benny and Jenny, chuckling. "Get it? Hare-y?"

Karl ignored the twins. "And this enraged bunny is **A THREAT TO CANADA?**"

Ron nodded. "**AND THE WORLD.**"

Mo cracked his knuckles. "So . . . all we have to do is grab him and lock him up again. What are we waiting for?"

Ron held up his hand. "That's no ordinary rabbit! It's got a vicious streak a mile wide!"

"**WE'VE DEALT WITH WORSE,**" said the twins.

"I can freeze it!" Karl said excitedly.

He made some snowflakes dance in the air. He'd only recently discovered he did indeed have a superpower — FREEZING STUFF — and he was eager to try it out in battle.

The twins began quietly humming "Let It Go," and Karl stopped and glared at them. They doubled down by singing, "Do You Want to Build a Snowman?" then had to leap out of the way as Karl fired a blast of ice their way.

Starlight had been lost in thought as the others confidently planned their easy triumph. She gave a little cough. "If I may interject with some observations," she said. The others turned her way. Starlight's "observations" were usually bang on. "We have **SEEN THE DAMAGE** that this **ONE RABBIT** has done to steel bars."

Ron projected the image of the **TWISTED CELL** the rabbit had escaped from.

Starlight held up a finger. "One, this is a rabbit with the **RAW POWER OF THE SQUAD OF ICE SQUIDS** we faced."

"And **DEFEATED**," Mo said.

Starlight held up two fingers. "Two, it has the **ABILITY TO BURROW UNDERGROUND**, moving in ways that we cannot. **LIKE THE ROBOTS WE FACED**."

"And **DEFEATED**," Mo said.

Starlight held up three fingers. "And, three, the bunny ALSO has **THE RAGE** of the **BRAINWASHED GECKOS** we faced."

"And **DEFEATED**," Mo said.

"I'm sensing a pattern," said DJ.

"DEFEAT!" said the twins, triumphantly.

DEFEAT!

"Yes. But we have not yet faced all these in combination. I've calculated the **PROBABILITY** of capturing such a beast, and those odds are almost **EXACTLY EVEN: FIFTY-FIFTY.**"

"Even odds. Sounds like a good nickname for the twins," said DJ with a chuckle.

"Odd for sure," said Karl.

"EVEN ODDS ARE GO!" The twins pumped their fists in the air. "Let's get that bunny!"

"Um," Ron said. "There's **ONE MORE THING** I haven't told you yet. The experiment also gave Mr. Fuzzywinkle the **ABILITY TO REASON . . . AND TALK.**"

CHAPTER TWO
IN FUR IT NOW

As the children were absorbing the latest news, Prime Minister Pauline Patinage was a few kilometres away, holding a silver shovel and trying to stay warm. Spring was in the air, but winter was holding on like a goalie with a loose puck.

"It's cold, Mr. Filbert," Patinage leaned over and whispered to her faithful assistant. "**BUT WE'RE DOING SOMETHING GOOD HERE TODAY.**"

"Agreed, PM PP." He chuckled at his favourite joke: PP.

Patinage frowned and pretended to threaten him with the shovel. He held up his hands in mock horror and they both laughed.

Now, there are many things politicians are known to shovel, but PM PP was holding this particular shovel as part of a photo op.

The PM was at the ground-breaking ceremony for a new hockey rink. But not just any hockey rink: ten ice pads, training rooms, a heated viewing area with gourmet food prepared by a famous chef. And the entire rink was going to be **POWERED BY THE GASSES COMING OFF DECOMPOSING HOCKEY EQUIPMENT.**

It was going to be GLORIOUS! Rink #10, the penthouse, was also going to be THE NEW SECRET TRAINING GROUND OF THE YOU KNOW WHOS. (Hint: there are six of them, and they are super. They are also kids. Did you figure it out?)

"I'm here today," the PM speeched, "to help usher in a **MORE EQUAL SPORTING WORLD**. We know how expensive hockey can be. Well, this rink will be made available to all — free of charge!"

The crowd cheered.

"And . . ." She paused for effect. "We will build one in each community in this great nation by the beginning of the next federal election."

The crowd of potential voters cheered again. Patinage waved, blew kisses to all the babies in the crowd, then held her shovel above the ground. Filbert motioned for the photographers to get ready.

Prime Minster Patinage, the Mayor of Tirabut, Quebec, and three local kids got ready to slide their shovels into the dirt.

THEY NEVER GOT THE CHANCE.

Just as Filbert said "Say cheese," the ground began to heave and roll like a wave on the ocean. The dignitaries and the kids fell down. So did Filbert and the photographers. **THERE WAS AN EXPLOSION OF DIRT, SPEWING LIKE A GEYSER.**

Cries for help rang out as a huge dust cloud obscured the area. **TWO LARGE PINK EARS SEEMED**

TO RISE UP WITH THE DEBRIS. Then, silence. The cloud began to dissipate like morning fog.

WHAT HAD HAPPENED?

All anyone knew for sure was that when the dust settled, the site had been swallowed up by a huge hole. **AND PRIME MINISTER PAULINE PATINAGE WAS NOWHERE TO BE FOUND.**

CHAPTER THREE
HARE-BRAINED

It was a naturally occurring sinkhole," Filbert said. He was sitting down in the Prime Minister's office, breaking the bad news to the Super Six.

"Stinkhole, you mean." Karl was livid. "**IT WAS MR. FUZZYWINKLE.**"

"Shhhhh!" Filbert nodded, looked around, and then spoke in a whisper. "We certainly suspect that. **BUT TO AVOID A PANIC, WE HAVE TO STICK TO THE SINKHOLE STORY**. Now, let's record your statement and we can send it out asap."

"Fine," Karl said. He stared into Filbert's phone and did his best to look sad.

"You should look like you've been crying," DJ said. He **GRABBED HIS WATER BOTTLE** 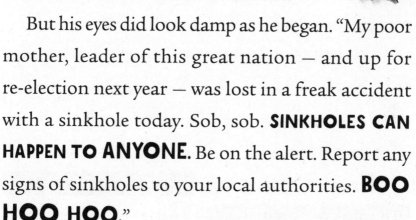 and sprayed Karl in the face.

"HEY!" Karl wiped most of the water away, but drips continued to slide down his cheeks. "Goalies! Sheesh!"

But his eyes did look damp as he began. "My poor mother, leader of this great nation — and up for re-election next year — was lost in a freak accident with a sinkhole today. Sob, sob. **SINKHOLES CAN HAPPEN TO ANYONE.** Be on the alert. Report any signs of sinkholes to your local authorities. **BOO HOO HOO.**"

"Good," Filbert said, stopping the recording. "I'll email that to our press secretary." He typed on his phone and there was a *whoosh* sound. "Sent."

DJ slow-clapped. "Get that Oscar acceptance speech ready, Karl."

Mo chuckled. **"YEAH. BEST ACTOR IN A TRAUMATIC HOLE."**

"Ha, ha. Whatever." Karl nodded. **"NOW, LET'S FIND MY MOM."**

"That's why we are in her office," Starlight said. She pushed a button on the PM's desk. Steel screens rolled down and covered the windows. Heavy bolts locked the doors. A screen dropped from the ceiling with a map of Canada.

"Um, we know we're in Canada," the twins said.

"Yes. But this is the `SECRET TRACKING SYSTEM FOR GUMPP`. And I'm betting that Karl's mom has a device on her."

Starlight tapped furiously on the keyboard. A red dot flashed on the screen. **"BINGO!"**

"Looks like they're moving into northern Quebec," DJ said.

"Time to move." Karl pushed a secret button on his tie clip. Instantly his clothes transformed into the red-and-white outfit of Captain Karl of the Super Six.

The others performed similar transformations.

Filbert clapped. **"THE SUPER SIX! THE HELICOPTER WILL MEET YOU ON THE ROOF IN TWO MINUTES."**

A secret door opened behind them, revealing the PM's secret elevator, which took them to the secret rooftop helicopter pad. Snow was beginning to whip up as they emerged on the roof. None of them felt the cold.

A dark blue helicopter slowly landed on a large painted number 6, a few metres away. Ron was in the pilot seat.

"Nice to have you along for the ride, good buddy," Mo said, as he began tossing the other five into their seats.

"Back at ya," Ron smiled. He wiped away a happy tear. His new friends were so much kinder than the evil boss he'd been serving in recent years. Lucky for them all, Clarence Crosscheck was now in jail with no chance of escape . . . At least not until, possibly, the next book. (Cue ominous music: **DA DA DA DAAAHHHHHH!!!**)

Starlight opened her laptop and clicked on the map. "They turned south."

"Buckle up!" Ron said.

The copter lifted off and **SPED TOWARD THE BLINKING RED DOT**.

But what was happening where **THAT RED DOT REALLY WAS . . . UNDERGROUND?**

ALL OF THE ACTION IS UNDER HERE!

That was just a test — but you'll probably want to get ready.

HA! HA! HA! HA! HA!

CHAPTER FUR
ARE YOU FUR REAL?

Put me down, you oaf!" yelled PM PP. She was being **HELD IN A VISE-LIKE GRIP** by the right hand of the giant bunny. With his left, the bunny was digging a tunnel with dazzling speed.

"SORRY!" Mr. Fuzzywinkle howled. **"I'M AFRAID YOU'RE COMING WITH ME."**

"YOU **CAN** TALK!"

"One of the side effects of the good doctor's treatment, yes. **I'M ALSO A GENIUS.** And I've been thinking about what I can do with all this new-found power and freedom."

"**YOU'LL NEVER SUCCEED.** The Super Six know I'm gone by now. And they'll be coming to save me."

Mr. Fuzzywinkle stopped digging for a second and turned on Patinage with a twisted smile. "I want them to."

And with an evil cackle, the bunny resumed his furious pace.

CHAPTER FIVE
FUR AWAY FROM HOME

The dot stopped moving. Starlight gasped. **"THEY'RE AT THE SECRET GUMPP ARMOURY!"**

"That's where only the most secret of secret and dangerous weapons are kept," DJ said. "Including all the experimental stuff taken from Crosscheck's lab."

The twins gasped.

Karl glared. "What is that bunny playing at? And why bring my mom?"

Starlight closed the laptop. "The bunny, and

your mom, are **UNDER** this facility."

"Under," Karl said angrily. "Of course. Where we can't get at them."

"What kind of hare-brained scheme is that bunny up to?" DJ asked. "Get it, hare-brained?"

The others groaned. Ron rolled his eye.

Ron landed the copter on the roof of the building. From the outside it looked just like an **ORDINARY HOCKEY STICK FACTORY**. But underneath and underground? It was an **IMPENETRABLE BUNKER**.

"There's no way that bunny can dig through. Those steel walls are **30 METRES THICK**," DJ said.

The others looked at him. "How do you always know this stuff?" Mo asked.

DJ tapped his helmet. "**I READ. I KEEP MY EYES OPEN. GOALIE SKILLS.**"

"So what do we do now?" asked the twins.

All eyes turned to Captain Karl. "Well, using Starlight's analysis, I say we could use a little help. I bet there are some things inside here that would come in handy."

"How are **WE** getting inside if the oversized bunny can't?"

"LUCKILY, AS USUAL, I'VE GOT A GREAT IDEA." Karl held up a shiny golden key.

"Isn't that the key you swiped to get us into **RINK 53**?" Mo asked.

"Sort of. It's a **MASTER KEY** that opens all GUMPP facilities. I made a copy in shop class."

He **BLASTED THE ROOF** with his hands, creating an **INSTANT ICE RINK**.

The twins immediately dropped a bucket of pucks and **BEGAN FIRING SHOTS** at DJ, who deflected most, missed one, and caught the rest.

"WE DON'T HAVE TIME TO PRACTISE!" Karl said.

The others looked at him, shocked.

"Okay," he said. "Three more shots. But then we go in. I just need to find the entrance."

"It's that thing," DJ said, pointing to a large steel box on the roof. "It looks like an air conditioning unit, but it's the door." He turned and saw the others looking at him. "What? I saw the blueprints on a **GUMPP FAN SITE** on the internet."

"Goalies," Karl said. He slid the key into the door and turned. There was the whir of hundreds of gears turning and the click of countless locks. After gathering up the loose pucks, the six kids jumped into the elevator and **PRESSED B.**

CHAPTER SIX
TIME FUR ANOTHER LOOK UNDERGROUND

W hy did we stop?" Patinage asked.

She and Mr. Fuzzywinkle (who, to save money on ink at the publisher's request, we will now refer to only as Fuzzy) had dug right up to the polished steel foundation of the building.

He dragged his claws along the metal, making a horrible scratching noise but leaving no mark at all on the metal.

"TITANIUM," he said, gazing at his claws. He flashed them at Patinage, who didn't flinch.

"IF YOU PLAN TO EAT ME, GET IT OVER WITH."

"I'M A VEGETARIAN," Fuzzy said, appearing shocked. "So unless you taste like a carrot, I'll pass."

"I don't. And YOU'RE NOT GETTING IN there with your claws or teeth," Patinage said.

"Be quiet," Fuzzy said.

Prime Minsiter Patinage had no intention of doing anything the bunny wanted, so she began singing "*Saute, saute, saute mon petit lapin*" in her loudest voice.

"Ha, ha," Fuzzy said dryly. He placed a giant paw over her mouth.

"*Mfmfmfm, gtrjhjknjhm ejfhjefh,*" Patinage continued, but almost no sound escaped the bunny's grip.

Fuzzy placed his left ear against the top of the tunnel and closed his eyes. After a few moments, his face broke into a huge smile. **"THEY HAVE ARRIVED."**

He turned to Patinage. "I'm afraid I've got to go. I've found some playmates who are more . . . bunny-ficial to my plans."

"What a horrible pun!"

Fuzzy sniffed indignantly, then dug a hole in the middle of the tunnel floor and dropped PM PP in. She tried to climb out, but the bunny was too fast, and in a flash, **SHE WAS BURIED UP TO HER NECK**.

"**YOU MONSTER**," she exclaimed.

"**DUH**." And with a final kick he covered her completely in dirt.

CHAPTER SEVEN
FUR HEAVEN'S SAKE

The elevator doors slid open with a "ding." Overhead lights flickered on, revealing a huge warehouse. One-hundred-foot-high metal shelves were covered from floor to ceiling with wooden crates labelled **"DANGER. EXPLOSIVES. BAD STUFF. DON'T TOUCH! OUCH!"**

At the far end, encased in shatterproof glass and protected by a lattice of laser beams, sat the only two **SIZEMATRON 2000s** known to exist.

"Still here!" the twins said.

"Good," Karl said. His shoulders relaxed. **"BUT THAT DEMENTED BUNNY IS COMING FOR THEM."** The bunny could have been after almost any technology, but Karl was now sure it was after the **SIZEMATRON 2000s**. "We need to **PROTECT THEM AT ALL COSTS**."

Starlight tapped her chin. "Are we one-hundred-percent sure this is what the bunny is after?"

Karl, who loved ALL of his ideas, felt a twinge of annoyance, but buried it. "Pretty sure. The bunny got angrier and stronger the bigger it got. It's here to get that **SIZEMATRON 2000** to get even bigger and even angrier."

"He'll be unstoppable," said the twins. "Like a huge, armed water ship!"

"We'll just have to bring that water ship down," DJ said.

Mo sighed. **"THAT BUNNY IS A TYPICAL BULLY."**

"Says the guy built like a brick wall," DJ laughed.

"STRENGTH ISN'T WHAT MAKES A BULLY. IT'S ATTITUDE."

"And if you're also tall, it's altitude," joked the twins.

"What a horrible pun. Look, I've dealt with a lot of bullies. They leave me alone now that I'm . . . well . . ." To demonstrate his point Mo flexed his biceps, stretching his jersey so much that the seams almost popped. "But they used to love picking on me."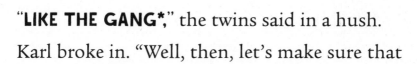

"LIKE THE GANG*," the twins said in a hush.

Karl broke in. "Well, then, let's make sure that

*The GANG are the school bullies and members of the GOOBERS school hockey team.

the **SIZEMATRON 2000s** don't fall into the wrong fuzzy hands." He blew on his fingers then pointed them at the floor.

"Last time I checked, bunnies can't skate." Karl activated his power and, **IN JUST A SECOND, THE ENTIRE SURFACE OF THE WAREHOUSE WAS A SMOOTH SHEET OF ICE.**

"**MORE PRACTICE TIME!!**" said the twins, and they began whipping all around the instant rink, shooting at DJ. He snared puck after puck — **UNTIL ONE SLAP SHOT** sailed a fraction of a fraction of a millimetre over his blocker.

"GOAL!" Jenny yelled. She and Benny gave each other a high-five.

DJ winced, expecting the sound of a smashing cinder block wall or exploding wooden storage. But there was only the **"POOF"** of the puck **HITTING SOMETHING SOFT**.

Karl's jaw fell open. The puck had banged off **THE FURRY, ALMOST VELVETEEN-SOFT, BELLY OF AN ENORMOUS RABBIT**, then rolled along the ice and was stopped by Starlight.

"Why, I think my little slippers just ran for cover," said Mr. Fuzzywinkle . . . . sorry . . . FUZZY. **AND THEN FUZZY CHARGED.**

CHAPTER EIGHT
FUR MINUTES BEFORE CHAPTER SEVEN

You're probably wondering **HOW FUZZY GOT INSIDE.**

Well, like this: Just after the Six left in the elevator, Ron sat staring at the controls of the copter, worried. The now blazing springtime sun had turned Karl's rooftop rink back into a puddle of water.

The **SURFACE RIPPLED SLIGHTLY.** A tiny wave lapped against the copter's landing skids.

"Odd," said Ron.

There was **ANOTHER, BIGGER RIPPLE,** and Ron felt a faint vibration in his feet. The copter swayed slightly. He flipped on his headset.

"Karl? It's Ron. Just checking in. All good?" His message was met by static. "Darn! The walls are too thick, even for GUMPP's technology. I better go see what's going on."

The helicopter **SHOOK WITH AN EVEN LOUDER VIBRATION** and the puddle rippled with huge waves. Ron grabbed the door handle to open the side door of the cockpit, but it wouldn't budge. He looked up. The window was filled with the sneering face of, you guessed it, a **GIANT BUNNY**.

"HELLO, RON," said Fuzzy with a grin. "Long time no see." He held up the mulched handle. "Tough to open a door without one of these. Unless, of course, you're super strong and can rip the metal off. Or pound it to dust."

He punched down on the helicopter roof, the dent stopping just short of Ron's head.

"MR. FUZZYWINKLE . . . FUZZY. WE SHOULD TALK!"

Fuzzy ripped off the nearest rotor and began whacking the front window. Huge cracks appeared.

Ron tried to fly to the other door, but just one glance showed that it was also handle-less.

The helicopter lifted into the air, which was odd because the engine was off.

"Bye, Ron," Fuzzy said, and he threw the copter off the edge of the building.

There was a **LOUD CRASH** as the copter fell to the ground, then **AN EXPLOSION** and **A PLUME OF ACRID BROWN SMOKE**.

"Now, time to join the others." Fuzzy slapped his hands together and bounded for the (thanks to Karl) unlocked elevator door.

CHAPTER NINE
FIVE MINUTES (AND FUR SECONDS) AFTER CHAPTER EIGHT

Turns out, you don't need to skate if you can slide super fast.

The Six were so shocked by Fuzzy's sudden appearance that they stood still for only a second. But it was long enough for **FUZZY TO PLOUGH INTO THE TWINS** as if they were bowling pins.

The impact slowed Fuzzy, and he stopped just short of the case containing the **SIZEMATRON 2000s**.

A LASER GRAZED HIS PAW, sending a puff of

smoke into the air. Fuzzy yelped and glared hard at the lasers. "Hmmm," he said quietly.

Jenny and Benny, meanwhile, sailed high in the air and over top of the shelving units.

Fuzzy smiled. "Split the uprights with those two. Three points. For me."

"Wrong game," Mo said, cracking his knuckles. He sped up and leaped at Fuzzy.

Fuzzy stood absolutely still until the last possible moment, then ducked as **MO TRIED TO GRAB FOR HIS EARS**.

Mo missed. "Oh no," he said as he flew straight toward the lasers.

Starlight, sensing the danger, acted quickly.

SHE SLAPPED THE PUCK STRAIGHT AT MO. It was slightly faster than his leap, and **HIT THE LASERS JUST AS HE DID**, making a hole in the deadly web.

"AHHHHHH!!!" Mo yelped in pain as an undeflected laser cut through his shoulder pads, but he passed through the dangerous beams mostly unscathed. His momentum carried him straight into the case.

The shatterproof glass was not, it turned out, MO-proof, and **THE CASE EXPLODED** on impact, sending shards of glass — **AND TWO SIZEMATRON 2000s** — skidding along the ice.

"Ha-ha!" Fuzzy yelled. **"SUCCESS!"**

One of the **SIZEMATRONS** smashed handle-first into the far wall, **EXPLODING IN FLAMES**. It sent a final blast of energy toward the hockey puck, making it so large it pinned Mo to the wall.

"NO!" Fuzzy yelled, watching the plume of smoke.

"DON'T LET THE RABBIT GET THE LAST ONE!" Starlight yelled.

Fuzzy, however, didn't move. Did he have a different plan? (HINT: Stay tuned!)

Mo used his stick to scoop the remaining gun. He passed it to DJ, who grabbed it and flipped it around, pointing it **DIRECTLY AT FUZZY**.

Only now did Fuzzy move. He furiously slapped his toes against the ice, gaining traction with each kick. **HE HEADED TOWARD KARL,** slowly at first, but then faster and faster.

"Bunny HUNGRY," he said.

"Yeah? Well, this hungry bunny bugs me." Karl dug his skates into the ice and **PREPPED FOR IMPACT**.

IT NEVER HAPPENED.

There was a gust of wind as the **TWINS ROUNDED THE STACKS AT FULL SPEED**. They'd found a long steel cable somewhere and raced toward Fuzzy.

CHAPTER TEN

TAKEN FUR A RIDE

Before we see what the twins had planned for Fuzzy, perhaps you've been wondering **WHAT HAPPENED TO RON AND PM PP?**

Does this burning wreck of the GUMPP helicopter answer your question?

How about this undisturbed pile of dirt, deep underneath the basement of the secret GUMPP armoury?

Totally (*sniff*) understand if (*sniff*) you need to take a second to weep before you turn the page (*sniff, sniff*).

Had a good cry? Composed enough to continue? Okay, turn the page . . .

CHAPTER ELEVEN
O FUR SIX

The twins spun around Fuzzy like a cyclone, wrapping the bunny in a **TIGHT COIL OF STEEL**.

"Oh no!" said Fuzzy. **"HOW CLEVER OF YOU!"** But why was he smiling?

"Stop whining, you furry menace," said the twins, winding the steel tighter and tighter.

Mo managed to shove away the charred remains of the giant puck and **JUMPED ON TOP OF THE BUNNY'S BACK**. Karl activated the super tape on his skates and took care of the bunny's legs. DJ held the **SIZEMATRON 2000** steady until Fuzzy was completely under wraps.

The Six stepped back to admire their handwork.

"Well, **THAT WAS EASIER THAN I THOUGHT** it would be," Karl said, poking the bunny's foot. **"NOW, WHERE'S MY MOM?"**

Fuzzy, instead of struggling or gnashing his teeth, began to giggle.

"Your mom is safe . . . if you consider being **BURIED ALIVE** safe!" The giggle turned into a laugh — a laugh eerily similar to Clarence Crosscheck's evil cackle.

Karl fell to his knees, tears filling his eyes. "NOOOOO!!!!"

Fuzzy laughed even louder and then started to rock back and forth. **HE ROCKED FASTER AND FASTER AND FASTER, AND THEN HE BEGAN TO ROLL.**

"Uh-oh," said Mo. He was thrown off the bunny and smashed into a box labelled "Stuff that will make you go OUCH!"

"OUCH!" he yelped.

Fuzzy rolled straight toward DJ.

"FIRE!" yelled the twins.

DJ raised the weapon and fired, pelting the rabbit's pelt with electric blue waves of energy.

Fuzzy twitched, and then **GREW AND GREW AND GREW**. His bulk strained at the cable, which began to fray, sending whips of steel flying around the room.

Two strips wrapped themselves around the twins, lashing them to the strut of a shelving unit.

"Oops," DJ said, then he was hit by a stray cable and sent sprawling across the floor.

"**TURN THE SWITCH THE OTHER WAY, YOU BONEHEAD!**" yelled the twins.

Fuzzy stomped toward DJ and raised his hands over his head, poised, it seemed, to mash him as flat as a pancake. But, for some reason, he stopped . . . and he looked to make sure DJ had **TURNED THE SWITCH TO "REVERSE."**

DJ had.

Fuzzy smiled.

Starlight realized **SOMETHING WAS FISHY**, but it wasn't until DJ raised the **SIZEMATRON 2000** again that she knew what it was.

"**STOP!**" Starlight yelled.

But DJ, thinking she was talking to Fuzzy,

didn't stop. He blasted the rabbit with a full dose of shrink ray.

Fuzzy began **TO SHRINK AND SHRINK AND SHRINK**. And as he did, he laughed.

"YOU FOOLS!" he said. "You've done what I could not, and now I am **TRULY UNSTOPPABLE!**"

"What?" DJ lowered the nozzle. "But you're just a normal cute bunny now."

"Don't call me **CUTE!!!**" Fuzzy yelled.

In a flash he was on DJ, boxing his helmet with his feet. Then Fuzzy grabbed the **SIZEMATRON 2000** from the goalie's loosened grip.

Fuzzy swung and pointed it at Mo, who was attempting to sneak up behind him with his hockey stick raised. "Move and you'll be so tiny you won't be able to lift a swizzle stick."

Mo stopped. Fuzzy began backing away into the elevator. Karl was still on his knees in shock. The twins struggled to escape their steel bonds.

Starlight glared at the retreating bunny. "**YOU WANTED TO BE SMALLER.**"

Fuzzy nodded. "Clever girl. **MUCH HARDER TO TRACK A REGULAR-SIZED BUNNY**, and much easier for me to lose myself in a crowd . . . or the ground."

"Why did he need us?" Karl asked.

Starlight glared at Fuzzy. "Because he couldn't do it himself."

"Even more clever. There was no way a bunny as large as me was breaking in here without help. Thanks, Karl."

Karl growled.

He held up his paw. "And even if I had made it this far, **MY OLD PAWS WERE MUCH TOO LARGE TO OPERATE THE SIZEMATRON 2000'S TRIGGER**. So I needed one of you to do that for me as well. Now, goodbye."

He backed into the elevator and the doors began to close. His paw appeared suddenly, and the doors slid open for a moment longer.

"Oh, and one more thing I should tell you. When you crossed those lasers **YOU ACTIVATED A SELF-DESTRUCT SEQUENCE FOR THE ARMOURY**. Which should have, if my calculations are right, about **10 SECONDS LEFT**."

The elevator doors closed.

And ten seconds later, **THE BUILDING ERUPTED IN A FIREBALL** that could be seen from a GUMPP base on the moon.

(How do we know this? You'll have to wait for the next book . . . **IF THERE IS A NEXT BOOK.** *Sniff, sniff.*)

CHAPTER TWELVE
NO TIME FUR BUNNY PUNS

Wondering **WHAT HAPPENED TO THE SUPER SIX?**

Does this trail of tiny rabbit tracks trailing away from this **SMOKING PILE OF RUBBLE** answer your question?

 Don't say you weren't warned that this book was sad.

But, now it's time for some more edumacating . . .

THIS LESSON IS ABOUT LOOKING *BEYOND* WHAT YOU SEE, AND TO KEEP ASKING QUESTIONS.

REMEMBER THOSE *DOES THIS ANSWER YOUR QUESTION?* QUESTIONS IN CHAPTER TEN? DID YOU ANSWER *YES?*

RON DELL **MUST** HAVE GONE DOWN WITH THE HELICOPTER. THE PILE OF DIRT **MUST** HAVE SUFFOCATED THE PM. AND THE SUPER SIX **MUST** BE INSIDE THE COLLAPSED BUILDING. RIGHT?

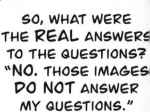

SO, WHAT WERE THE **REAL** ANSWERS TO THE QUESTIONS? "NO. THOSE IMAGES DO NOT ANSWER MY QUESTIONS."

BUT, THIS IS THE DANGER OF *JUMPING TO CONCLUSIONS* WITHOUT *EVIDENCE*. DID YOU DRAW CONCLUSIONS QUICKLY WITHOUT ASKING MORE QUESTIONS? ALWAYS KEEP ASKING QUESTIONS!!! LIKE . . . DID YOU ACTUALLY SEE RON IN THE WRECKAGE?

THIS IS A PROBLEM WITH MANY TYPES OF QUESTIONS. YOU ALMOST ALWAYS HAVE INSUFFICIENT INFORMATION TO ANSWER THEM ACCURATELY RIGHT AWAY.

? ? YES? NO? ? ?

$2 + 2 = ?$

DO YOU KNOW THE ANSWER TO THIS ONE?

A: ___ ?

ANSWER: IF YOU THOUGHT 4, YOU ARE RIGHT AND WRONG. YES, 2 PLUS 2 EQUALS 4. BUT WHAT IF YOU WERE ADDING 2 CATS AND 2 BIRDS? ANSWER? 2.

2 **WELL-FED** CATS.

MORE INFORMATION HELPS YOU GET BETTER ANSWERS. STAY CURIOUS. AVOID MAKING SNAP JUDGMENTS. DON'T LET PEOPLE TRICK YOU!

SO WHAT DID ACTUALLY HAPPEN? LET'S FIND SOME ANSWERS TO OUR EXTRA QUESTIONS.

CHAPTER THIRTEEN
SOME ANSWERS FUR YOU

Well, as you can see, Starlight and Karl are **NOT DEAD**. Are Ron and PM PP? Stay tuned.

Let's start with the fate of the Super Six. When we last saw them, they were **INSIDE A BUILDING WITH A TICKING TIME BOMB.**

DJ was dizzy. The twins were tied up. Mo was attempting to pry open the elevator doors. They were doomed.

So it seemed a safe assumption that they'd be blown up or burned to a crisp. But what Fuzzy had not counted on was the combination of Starlight's brain, Karl's amazing superpowers, **AND SALIVA.**

So . . . let's jump back into the scene **RIGHT BEFORE THE BOOM.**

"**FIVE** SECONDS LEFT!" screamed the twins.

FIVE SECONDS LEFT!

Starlight grabbed DJ and hugged the twins. "Mo! Here now. Karl! **FREEZE DOME!**" Starlight yelled.

Karl leaped to her side and raised his hands above his head. A split second later **THE ENTIRE BUILDING WAS ENGULFED IN FLAMES.** BUT Karl had successfully formed a giant ice ball around himself and his five friends. The **SUPER FREEZING SNAPPED THE CABLES** that held the twins, and Benny and Jenny fell at Karl's feet.

"Nice job, captain!" they cheered. But the jubilation was short lived as the **IMMENSE HEAT BEGAN TO MELT THE ICE**.

"**I NEED MORE WATER!**" Karl hissed through gritted teeth.

Starlight looked around frantically for a water bottle, but they had all been left behind in the copter. Her mind raced, and then her eyes grew wide. "**EVERYONE! SPIT!!!!!**"

DJ woke from his stupor. "You have got to be kid—"

"**SPIT!!!**"

The air was soon filled with saliva. Karl gathered the slobber and froze it to the inside walls of the ball.

"I thought a spitball was only in baseball," DJ laughed.

Karl was doing his best to keep the flames at bay. But the intense heat continued to eat away at the crust. "**WE GOTTA GET AWAY FROM HERE!**"

"**EVERYONE SKATE!**" Starlight yelled over the roar of the flames.

With all six churning their feet, the ball spun faster and faster and faster. The ball created its own fire tornado as it began to rise **HIGHER AND HIGHER.**

Cracks appeared. Small flames crept through, licking Karl's fingers.

"**WE NEED MORE SPIT!**"

"There's none left!" Mo said in a croak.

Karl strained to keep the ball together.

"She can't take any more, captain!" yelled the kids.

There was a **GIANT BOOM** as the fire below hit some explosives. The blast sent the remains of the ball, with the Six inside, **HURTLING THROUGH THE AIR**. They hit the ground with a crack, then a splash, safely away from the collapsed armoury.

"WELL, THAT WAS DRAMATIC," said a voice.

Karl looked up. "RON!"

Yes, and Ron was holding the hand of a dirt-covered PM PP.

CHAPTER FOURTEEN
HOW WE GOT HARE

So, that didn't exactly work out great," Karl said, lying down on the cool grass. Smoke from the nearby fire filled the sky.

He'd just filled in his mom on Fuzzy's latest escape. She brushed some loose dirt off her shoulders and spoke. "It could have been WAY worse. **ANY IDEA WHAT FUZZY IS UP TO?**"

"About thirty-five centimetres," DJ joked.

Starlight rolled her eyes. "**HE DID WANT TO BE BUNNY-SIZED AGAIN.**"

"And we helped him do it," the twins said sadly.

"But what can one little bunny do better than one **GIANT** monster bunny?" Karl asked.

"Hide and escape," said Starlight.

They sat in silence for a long time.

"Why are you two so dirty?" Mo asked Patinage and Ron.

"He buried me alive," the Prime Minister said.

"And he threw me off the building inside a helicopter."

Mo shook his head. "See! A rabbit-sized rabbit, no matter how strong, can't do either of those things!"

Karl hugged his mom. **"AND HOW DID YOU TWO ESCAPE?"**

"I still have a few tricks up my sleeve," Ron said.

He closed his fingers together, **FORMING A SHARP POINT, LIKE THE EDGE OF AN AXE**. "I finished busting the front window and leaped out just before the copter hit the ground. Simple."

All eyes swivelled to Patinage.

"My glasses. They also have a **BUILT-IN OXYGEN MASK**. If you breathe slowly through your nose, there's enough compressed air to sustain a person for about twenty minutes."

Starlight cocked her head. "But you couldn't move enough to dig yourself out, could you?"

"No. That's thanks to Ron."

Ron blushed. "I saw that Fuzzy didn't have your mom when he jumped on the roof, so I knew she was in danger. I **ACTIVATED MY COMM LINK—**" He pressed a button on his head and the Six heard a squawk in their headsets. "You Six didn't hear inside those thick walls. But the PM heard me."

"And I was able to tell Ron where I was. Even with my mouth full of dirt." She dug a pebble out from between her teeth and spat.

"I followed Fuzzy's big footprints back to a big hole. I jumped down and dug her out." He flattened his hands, turning them into trowels.

Patinage nodded. **"LUCKILY, WE RAN AWAY JUST BEFORE THE BUILDING BLEW."**

Karl wiped a frozen tear from his eye. "Thank you, Ron."

Ron beamed.

Mo stood up and stretched his muscles. "Now, let's find out where that bunny hopped off to."

"And then," said the twins, **"WE PUT HIS NOT-SO-FUNNY BUNNY BUTT IN JAIL."**

CHAPTER FIFTEEN
HOPPING TO IT

The bunny-sized Fuzzy's tracks led to a nearby field.

DJ was the first to spot the hole. He stuck his goalie stick in as far as it would go, which wasn't far. He turned to the others. "It's not deep."

Mo put his ear to the ground, **THEN PUNCHED THE EARTH SO HARD THE TREES SHOOK.**

"Barely an echo.

It's only hollow for a few feet. Then it's solid ground again."

"It doesn't matter." Starlight shook her head. "There's no way we could fit inside to follow him. ANOTHER ADVANTAGE OF BEING A SMALL EVIL BUNNY."

"Small tunnels." Karl growled.

"SO, HOW DO WE FIND HIM AND CATCH HIM?" asked the twins.

PM PP waved a finger in the air. "He must have a larger plan. Something he needed the SIZEMATRON 2000 for. We may just have to be patient and wait for him to show himself."

Ron shuddered. "By then it may be too late."

Their conversation was interrupted by the sound of Mr. Filbert pulling up in a large truck. The Six plus Ron plus PM PP got in silently, each thinking their own thoughts. (Of course they were. Have you ever tried thinking someone else's thoughts? Way too hard.)

But, they did all share one huge question: **WHERE WAS FUZZY?**

Perhaps **YOU** were asking yourself the same thing?

Does this picture of a giant chicken answer your question?

TRICKED YOU!

This time the picture actually **DOES** answer the question.

Because what Fuzzy had done was dig right up under a farm in the rolling foothills of the Laurentians. And he'd just **ZAPPED AN OLD ENGLISH GAME ROOSTER** named Corncob.

And Corncob was not happy about it. He was so unhappy, in fact, that he was pecking the metal roof of the building that butted up against his pen.

It helped that Fuzzy had thrown some kernels of corn onto the roof to make sure Corncob pecked a lot. **WHY HAD FUZZY DONE THIS, YOU ASK?** (See how good you are getting at asking follow-up questions!)

Well, because the building was filled with . . . **BUNNY RABBITS!** And not just any rabbits, but one rabbit in particular. See, this was where Fuzzy grew up, and fell in love.

"I'm coming, Petunia," Fuzzy said.

Corncob ripped a bigger and bigger hole in the roof. Then a pair of dark rabbit ears appeared, twitching in the wind.

Fuzzy took aim at Corncob and fired. An electric blue streak whacked the rooster in the side, instantly shrinking him back down to the size of an ordinary rooster. Corncob, no longer enraged, began pecking at the ground calmly.

Fuzzy looked back to the roof and smiled. The pair of ears had been followed through the hole by a twitching nose, and **NOW A DOE***, whose eyes locked on Fuzzy.

"Petunia," Fuzzy said. He choked up. **"HOW I'VE MISSED YOU."**

Petunia ran around the edge of the roof looking for a way down.

"Jump, my darling!" Fuzzy said. "And I will catch you."

She did. He did.

They hugged. Then Fuzzy stepped aside, **REVEALING HIS BOX OF WRISTBANDS**.

"These are what made me the bunny I am today. **BRILLIANT! POWERFUL!** With them we could rule the world. **WILL YOU JOIN ME?**"

Petunia nodded, and held out her arm.

----

*The name for a female rabbit. You are learning SO MUCH!

Fuzzy handed her a wristband. **SHE TIED IT ON AND BEGAN TO SHAKE.**

"Petunia? Are you okay?" Fuzzy asked, lips trembling.

Petunia stopped shaking quickly, and looked up at her true love. "I have never felt better," she said. "Now, my sweet, what shall we do next?"

CHAPTER SIXTEEN
GONE TOO FUR

The next few weeks were quiet. **TOO QUIET.** The Six went to school, got taunted by the GANG, did their best to practise some secret hockey at **RINK 53** . . . and waited for Fuzzy to tip his hand, or more accurately, his foot.

BUT NOTHING HAPPENED.

"Boooooring," DJ said as they cooled down after a particularly tiring practice.

Mo looked up from untying his skates. "What are you talking about? **WE'VE HAD SOME MISSIONS.**"

"Call those missions!?" DJ scoffed. "Even a group of forwards could have handled those bees."

"Wasps," Starlight said. "Mechanical wasps."

Yes, the Six had battled and defeated a team of **CHAINSAW-WIELDING ROBOT WASPS**. The wasps had been programmed by a greedy hockey stick manufacturer to attack a rival's warehouse in Northern Manitoba.

Karl smiled. "I did love the way they exploded when they hit that giant wall of ice we made."

"And we took some amazing jumps off that thing to whack the leader," the twins said, slapping hands.

"Yeah," Mo said. "And what about the pirates we had to stop?"

"Okay, that was pretty cool," said DJ.

Yes, the Six had also battled a group of **PIRATES WHO'D DISGUISED THEMSELVES AS THE VANCOUVER CANUCKS** to steal a shipload of wild salmon.

"Nice work on that one, Starlight," Karl said.

Starlight waved away the compliment. "It was easy to calculate the right trajectory for the puck barrage. I just needed to take into account the speed of the tanker ship they'd hijacked, along with the curvature of the Earth." She paused and tapped her chin. "Although the inconsistent wind speed off English Bay was a variable I had to make some slight . . ." She stopped. The locker room had gone silent. "What?"

"You are just impressive," Karl said with an awed look.

"And maybe a little scary," said the twins.

"Scary smart," DJ said. "Like one of those atomic manatees I've read about."

"Thanks, DJ," Starlight said.

"I just shot the pucks as hard as I could," Mo said.

"And it worked," said Starlight patting his knee pad. "**WE ARE A TEAM AND WE WORKED TOGETHER AND THAT'S WHAT MATTERS.**"

"The Hockey Super Six!" they cheered.

DJ chugged some water. "Hey, Karl. I thought your mom said we had to be on the lookout for some network of evil or something."

Karl shrugged. "The androids have been out for months now and haven't seen any sign. Maybe Crosscheck was working alone?"

DJ gave a deep sigh. "That guy was a jerk. But it was kinda fun to beat him."

Mo smirked. "**YEAH. HE WAS A CHALLENGE.**"

PM PP walked into the locker room. "You MAY remember that he also tried to destroy the country and turn all the schools into robot factories."

The twins smiled. "Good times."

"**HE WAS A TRUE RIVAL,**" said Starlight. "Of course, we didn't have mind-controlling devices strapped onto our *articulatio radiocarpalis*, like Karl did."

"I assume that means wrist?" Karl asked. Starlight nodded. "Well, I can tell you that it's not fun. Your brain gets bombarded with information, all with Crosscheck's creepy voice . . . Wait!" Karl sat bolt upright.

"What's wrong?" asked the others.

Karl didn't answer, but pressed a button on his helmet and **RE-WATCHED THE RECORDING OF THEIR ENCOUNTER IN THE ARMOURY**. And he saw it. "**LOOK AT THIS!**"

He projected the image onto the wall. "**FUZZY WASN'T THERE JUST FOR THE SIZEMATRON 2000.**" He pointed at the tiny box tucked away in the back of the elevator — a box **FILLED WITH MIND-CONTROLLING WRISTBANDS**.

Patinage whistled. "He's going to use those. But on who or what?"

Starlight turned to Ron. "Those don't by any chance **CONTAIN TRACKING CHIPS**, do they?"

Ron didn't answer, but he pressed his left tooth. His stomach instantly turned into a map of Canada. And **THE MAP WAS FILLING IN WITH MOVING RED DOTS,** spreading out like an exploding firework.

At that exact moment, Patinage's comm link was bombarded with numerous **REPORTS OF SINKHOLES, ALL OF THEM UNDERNEATH CANADA'S RICHEST GOLD RESERVES.**

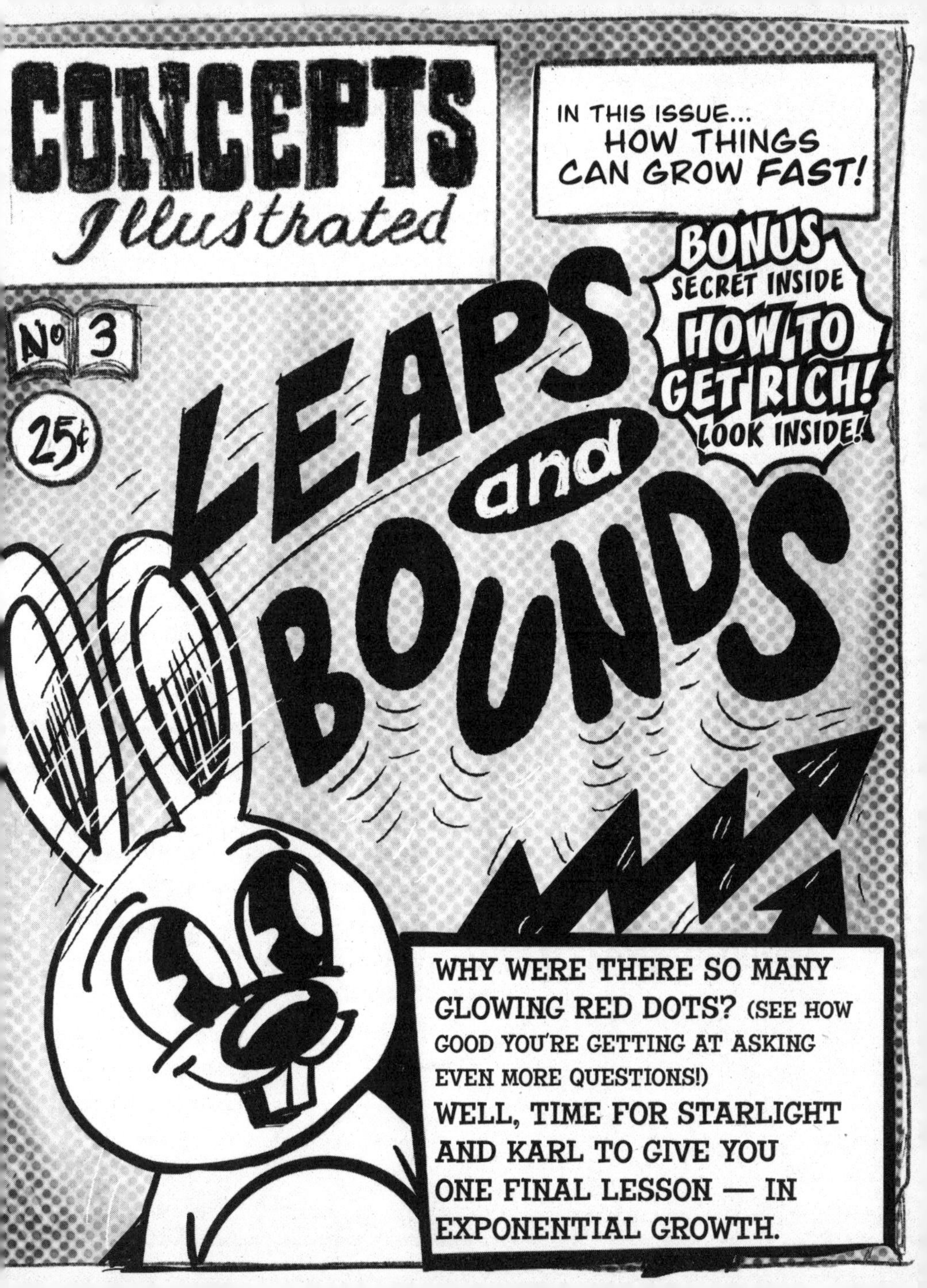
CONCEPTS
Illustrated
IN THIS ISSUE...
HOW THINGS
CAN GROW FAST!
BONUS
SECRET INSIDE
HOW TO
GET RICH!
LOOK INSIDE!
No 3
25¢
LEAPS
and
BOUNDS
WHY WERE THERE SO MANY GLOWING RED DOTS? (SEE HOW GOOD YOU'RE GETTING AT ASKING EVEN MORE QUESTIONS!)
WELL, TIME FOR STARLIGHT AND KARL TO GIVE YOU ONE FINAL LESSON — IN EXPONENTIAL GROWTH.

CHAPTER SEVENTEEN
HARE AND THERE

How many gold reserves were attacked?" Patinage yelled into her comm link.

Filbert's voice came back through the earpiece. "A hundred! **ALL OF THE VAULTS 'POOF!' DISAPPEARED** into the ground. **LIKE MAGIC.**"

"What does a bunny need gold for!?" PM PP wailed.

"Most of the sinkholes are clustered around here," Ron said, looking down at his tummy and pointing at the Ontario-Quebec border.

Starlight watched the moving dots. "They seem to be **MOVING AWAY FROM THE POINTS OF IMPACT**."

"It's the classic flight reaction," DJ said. "I used to raise rabbits."

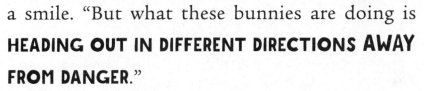

"Real ones?" joked the twins. "Or imaginary nuclear ones?"

"Both." DJ didn't even crack a smile. "But what these bunnies are doing is **HEADING OUT IN DIFFERENT DIRECTIONS AWAY FROM DANGER**."

Starlight began tracing the path of each bunny, backwards.

"That tickles!" said Ron.

Starlight turned to the others. "DJ's right. There's a pattern. They all started in one central place, halfway between Montreal and Toronto, and then fanned out."

They could all see it now. Different clusters of red dots were heading east, some west, some north, **BUT ALL AWAY FROM A CENTRAL POINT.**

"What are we waiting for?" Karl said. "**LET'S GO GRAB THEM!**"

"Wait." Starlight shook her head. "There's no way we can grab them all at once."

"I bet we can!" said the twins.

"We'll **SPLIT UP** and try to corral as many as we can," said Karl.

"We call Manitoba!" said the twins. "We love Winnipeg!"

Mo touched the red 6 on his jersey. "Split up the Super Six? **DOES THAT SEEM WISE?**"

"No," Starlight admitted. "And it is perhaps exactly what Fuzzy wants us to do."

"Meaning?" asked the dejected twins.

"His bunnies are only mimicking a flight response, trying to trick us into attacking separately, and very far apart. I'm willing to bet that Fuzzy is sitting at the starting point like a general at command central."

DJ smiled. "And he knows we can be beaten if we're split up."

"SO LET'S NOT FALL INTO HIS TRAP."

"We go for the head," DJ said.

"Instead of the unlucky feet," the twins said.

PM PP spoke into her comm link. "Mr. Filbert? Send a stealth helicopter ASAP. It's very, very quiet. We're going rabbit hunting."

CHAPTER EIGHTEEN
BONUS EDUCATIONAL IN-FUR-MATION

Okay, one last pause to cram a last bit of useful stuff into your brain. It's something called **"FORESHADOWING."** If you haven't learned it in school yet, you will. Either way, you'll learn it now.

Storytellers use this all the time to hint, tease, maybe even trick, the people who hear or read their stories. That **BUILDS TENSION**. As in, "Oh no! I sense bad things are about to happen! How will they escape?" And foreshadowing is almost always about bad stuff.

You ever watch a horror movie and the main character says, "We'll be safe in there!" and they point at the spookiest-looking house? You know that's not going to go well. Or a kid in a movie or book says, "This vacation is going to be the best ever!" There's a one hundred percent chance it won't be.

So when Starlight says **THEY AREN'T GOING TO FALL INTO FUZZY'S "TRAP"** of chasing a bunch of marauding baby bunnies across the map of Canada, **WHAT DO YOU THINK IS REALLY GOING TO HAPPEN?**

Do you think someone was planning this all along? Fuzzy? Was he?

 Get those tissues ready.

CHAPTER NINETEEN
THE EYE OF THE FUR-ICANE

Ron lowered the copter into a clearing, near the Belleponte truck stop. The lake sparkled in the distance under a clear blue sky. Everything seemed perfectly ordinary on the surface.

Drivers on their way to or from the big cities shared the same look of disappointment as they sipped their bad coffee and chewed doughnuts that tasted like glue. But the Six knew that underneath, somewhere, was a bunny rabbit bent on spreading **CHAOS AND DESTRUCTION.**

The copter's rotors came to a stop. PM PP's voice squawked over the speaker. "Ron, I'd like this copter back, please."

"I'll do my best," Ron said.

"Okay, my hockey superheroes," Patinage said to the kids. "**GUMMP DRONES ARE ON THEIR WAY** to intercept the bunnies. **FIND FUZZY.** Copy?"

"COPY!" They slipped out of the copter and got ready to look for the entrance to Fuzzy's underground lair. **RON BEGAN ROLLING AROUND** the parking lot in smaller and smaller circles. To an outside observer he looked like a spare tire that had come loose from the back of a passing jeep.

"What is he doing?" DJ asked, watching Ron start to slow down.

"Depth sounder," Starlight said. "We made some adjustments to Ron's internal sensors. He can now **USE SONAR TO SENSE IF THERE'S A TUNNEL UNDERGROUND**."

"Cool!" said the twins.

Ron's spinning ended **NEAR AN OLD ORANGE MINI CAR**. "He's under here."

Starlight wheeled around the truck. "All four tires are flat. There's even grass growing up from under them."

"Meaning?" DJ asked.

"**THE CAR IS A DECOY**," said Starlight. "Placed here a while ago **TO COVER SOMETHING**."

"The front door, I bet," said Karl.

"On it," Mo said. He lifted the car. Underneath? **A HOLE IN THE PAVEMENT.**

Karl nodded. "I'd say about the size of two demented bunny rabbits hopping side by side."

"I'll go tell the PM," Ron said.

"We need to open that door a bit more," Starlight said.

"On it," said DJ. He took his **GOALIE STICK AND BEGAN CHURNING IT IN A CIRCLE**. Asphalt, concrete and dirt spun through the air, forming a circular mound around the kids. After only a minute he'd dug a pit about three metres deep.

"I wondered if that would work!" DJ said, smiling proudly.

"Remind me never to skate through your crease," Mo joked.

"Never skate through my crease."

"Why'd you stop?" Starlight asked.

"Rock. I was able to chip at it a bit, but **I CAN'T DIG THROUGH**." He pointed to a cracked surface of pinkish granite.

"Looks like your brain," the twins joked.

"Please . . . skate through my crease," DJ said, narrowing his eyes and tapping the blade of his stick into his glove.

"We're here to fight a bunny rabbit, remember?" Karl said, jumping into the hole. "Not each other."

Karl grabbed a water bottle from his belt (a uniform addition Starlight had suggested after the armoury debacle) and covered the stone with water.

"**WHAT A WASTE!**" said DJ.

"What's he gonna do?" asked the twins.

Karl waited to let the **WATER SEEP INTO THE CRACKS**. Then he knelt down and placed his hands on the stone. The water **FROZE, THEN EXPANDED, WIDENING THE CRACKS AND SPLITTING THE ROCK.**

Starlight grinned. "The same effect causes cracks in mountainsides, glaciers, sidewalks, roads . . ."

"We got it," said the twins.

Karl stood back up again. "Now I just **WAIT FOR IT TO THAW**, then it seeps deeper down. DJ?"

DJ spun his goalie stick like a fan, creating a warm wind.

"Thanks!" Karl said.

Karl froze the water again. "I keep doing this until I crack this rock wide open and we see what's underneath."

"It's like a huge Kinder Surprise egg!" said the twins.

"Except I bet the bunny down there ain't handing out chocolates," DJ said.

Two more freeze-and-thaw cycles and the stone began to fall down in chunks.

"As I suspected," Karl said. "It's hollow und—" He didn't finish the sentence, because in a flash **THE ENTIRE FLOOR CAVED IN,** and **THE SUPER SIX SLID DOWN THE SIDES OF A WIDE HOLE, STRAIGHT INTO A STEEL CAGE.**

A steel lid clanged closed above them and the Super Six were thrown into darkness.

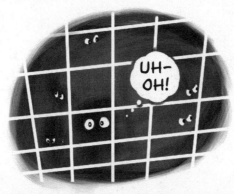

UH-OH!

CHAPTER TWENTY
YOU FELL FUR IT!

I expected so much more," said a voice in the gloom.

Lights flickered on, revealing the face of — you guessed it — Fuzzy. He was seated in a tiny swivel chair, twirling around and around. Petunia was nearby, nose twitching, her hand typing away on a laptop. **"The children are on their way to the rendezvous point, darling,"** she said, closing the computer and tucking it into a backpack.

"DID THEY DROP THE GOLD AND WRISTBANDS?" Fuzzy asked.

"Of course!" Petunia said with a smile. "Just like we asked them. I'll go get some carrots ready for the trip. Hot springs sound so lovely at this time of year!"

"One more thing," said Fuzzy. He **PULLED A BLACK WRISTBAND** out of Petunia's backpack. He pushed a button and the wristband began to blink red. "Drop this in the truck up top. That way the drones . . . **AND THE MISSILES . . . CAN FIND IT**."

Petunia gave Fuzzy a peck on the cheek and hopped down the tunnel into the dark, the red light of the wristband getting fainter and fainter until it disappeared.

"You don't want the gold?" Karl asked.

Fuzzy turned his attention back to the kids. "What use would I have for gold? I can dig up as much as I want down here. No. **THE GOLD, AND THE WRISTBANDS, WILL SOON BE BLOWN UP TO TEACH YOU A LESSON.** That's all."

"**MISSILES?**" Mo asked.

"What do you think those GUMPP drones Patinage sent out are going to do? They aren't armed with **CUTE LITTLE BUNNY NETS.** She just told you they were going to 'intercept' the others." He pointed at his ears. "**I HEAR EVERYTHING.**"

The Six were speechless. Could he be right?

Fuzzy laughed. "How ironic that they will vaporize the very gold you greedy humans love so much. **OH, AND YOU SIX WILL GET VAPORIZED TOO.**" He pointed up to the surface where Petunia was at that moment dropping the blinking wristband.

"YOU MONSTER!" Starlight hissed through the cage. Her eyes darted around the room **LOOKING FOR ANYTHING THAT COULD HELP** them escape.

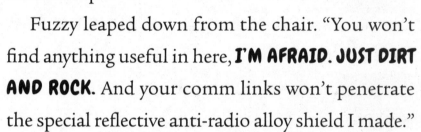

Fuzzy leaped down from the chair. "You won't find anything useful in here, **I'M AFRAID. JUST DIRT AND ROCK.** And your comm links won't penetrate the special reflective anti-radio alloy shield I made."

He began hopping around the front of the cage. "Victory IS sweet. Like a giant carrot!"

"You haven't won yet," Mo said with a scowl.

"Says the boy in the cage." Fuzzy laughed. "Oh, how **CROSSCHECK WOULD RANT AND RAVE ABOUT YOU SIX. ALL. THE. TIME**. It made me wonder how powerful you must be! How wrong I was."

Karl blasted Fuzzy with his fingers. There was a smash of exploding glass, and Fuzzy reappeared a few metres away.

"MIRRORS," Fuzzy said. "A trick I learned from El Slapo. But by all means, try again."

Karl blasted and blasted, each time shattering another mirror, and each time **MISSING THE REAL FUZZY**.

Fuzzy shook his head. "I can't see how Crosscheck could lose to you all so easily."

"You're just like him," Mo said.

"No. I'm much better. You see, I heard all the plans and plots that he came up with. And how they all failed."

"How we beat him, you mean," Karl said.

Fuzzy cackled. "No. He defeated himself, really. He was too confident."

"HA!" laughed the twins.

"It's true! He **OVERESTIMATED YOU** and, subsequently, **IGNORED YOUR MANY, MANY WEAKNESSES.**"

"What do you mean, weaknesses?" asked Starlight.

"Ironically, the same things you think are your strengths: Power, speed, smarts. Let me tell you a story."

"Ugh," said the twins.

"Ron, that simpleton, thought it might distract me from my prison conditions if I were allowed to **WATCH HOCKEY GAMES.** So he set up a TV, far enough that I couldn't reach but close enough that I could catch all the action. **AND I LEARNED A LOT.**"

"Like what?" asked Karl, blasting yet another mirror image of their tormentor.

"THE CARDINAL RULE I LEARNED," Fuzzy continued, "is that it's not always the most skilled team or the best athletes who win. The truly great teams, the truly great players, **ALWAYS USE THE OTHER TEAM'S AGGRESSION AGAINST THEM.**"

"Aggression? Like fighting?" Mo asked.

"Nothing so barbaric or simple," Fuzzy said. "What happens is that overconfident players **RELY TOO MUCH** on their natural skills. And that makes them all too eager to jump straight into a game **WITHOUT DOING ALL THE PREPARATION** necessary to be truly strong, truly prepared, truly a team. Sound like anyone you know?"

"What the heck is this demented bunny prattling on about?" DJ turned to Starlight. "Starlight is always doing thinking stuff in her head to think about thinking more stuff."

"Clearly you don't," Fuzzy said, wagging a dismissive paw at DJ.

DJ growled. "This radioactive bunny is starting to bug me."

"YOU'RE TALKING ABOUT JUMPING TO CONCLUSIONS," Starlight said, hanging her head.*

Fuzzy beamed. "Starlight knows what I'm talking about. **SHE LOOKS FOR PATTERNS.** That's how her brain works. But she looks **TOO QUICKLY.** So I created a pattern for my children to display, which led you straight to me."

Starlight smacked her own helmet. "I was so stupid!"

Fuzzy smiled. "You calculated that, even if I were here and armed,

---

*She should have paid more attention to chapter 12!

you still had a better chance beating me if you were together."

"Better than trying to stop all your scattered bunnies. Yes."

"Which seemed like a wise decision. Except you ignored the possibility that I had no intention of fighting at all AND that my children were not really running away with the gold. The result? You Six literally leaped right into your very own penalty box."

Mo tried to rip the steel bars apart, but despite quivering slightly they remained in place.

"Tsk, tsk, tsk," Fuzzy wagged a paw. "Not this cage, my colossal fellow. You may recognize it. Crosscheck **KEPT A WHOLE TEAM OF MARAUDING ICE**

SQUIDS LOCKED INSIDE FOR WEEKS. And they never even dented the bars."

"The cage from **RINK 53**." Mo slumped down to his knees.

Fuzzy rocked on his legs. "I've won. Think of it like a hockey game. **YOU PUSH TOO HARD, ACT TOO QUICKLY, AND YOU MAKE MISTAKES.**"

"We don't make mistakes," the twins said through clenched teeth.

"Really? Go back and rewatch the game against the robots. I did, a hundred times. You two had better options available, all game long. Karl was wide open. You didn't pass. PM PP was alone in front of the net? You shot instead. Even when Starlight TOLD you to stop skating so fast, you just couldn't help yourselves."

The twins sulked but said nothing.

"I won't bore you with more details of **ALL YOUR VARIOUS SHORTCOMINGS**. Suffice it to say that each of you has many. Like Karl, who keeps wasting all the moisture down here with useless attempts to catch me off guard."

As if on cue, Karl's fingers stopped blasting. His lips felt dry and he slid against the bars and onto the floor.

The real Fuzzy stepped out from the shadows. "You all need to **THINK MORE BEFORE ACTING**. Oh! And I need to move before the missiles start falling."

He waved at the Six and then hopped toward the darkness.

"But . . . why?" Starlight called after him. "Why do all this? Revenge?"

Fuzzy stopped and turned over his shoulder.

"Just revenge? If so I'd be attacking Crosscheck. No. **IT'S NOT JUST REVENGE. IT'S SAVING THE WORLD.** Humans have been wreaking havoc on this planet for far too long. **NOW PREPARE FOR THE AGE OF THE BUNNY!**"

He disappeared.

"He's got a point, you know," said DJ.

"Many," Starlight added with a sigh.

They sat thinking about what Fuzzy had said, and done, for what seemed like ages. Mo tried again and again to rip apart the bars, with no luck. Starlight sat quietly, looking for anything in the tunnel they could use to escape the cage. **BUT IT WAS KARL WHO FINALLY BROKE THE SILENCE:** "Team, I have an idea."

CHAPTER TWENTY-ONE
IT'S YOUR FUR-NERAL

Karl cocked an ear down the tunnel. "Anyone hear the padding of hundreds of tiny feet?" he asked.

"Nope," said the others.

"So presumably, **FUZZY'S CHILDREN ARE NOT COMING BACK HERE**. Good. No one gets hurt."

Starlight cocked an ear. "**AND, SO FAR, NO MISSILES BLOWING UP.**"

Mo kept trying to bend the bars, and failed. "So, what's your great idea to get us out of here, cap?"

Karl knelt down on the floor. "**FUZZY ACTUALLY**

GAVE US ALL THE DETAILS WE NEED TO KNOW. He said this was the cage the Ice Squids were kept in."

"Kept being the operative word here, captain," Mo said, trying, and failing, one more time to pry the bars apart.

Karl grabbed his water bottle and splashed a puddle onto the floor. He began waving his hands in the air. Slowly he formed what seemed to be an ice cream cone. "It's very delicate, so **SHHHHHH** everyone."

Karl leaned his mouth close to the cone and whispered, "Klort? Splort? Blort? Remember us?" He leaned his ear against the cone. For a moment he was perfectly still, then he smiled and nodded and spoke into the cone again.

"Splort! Nice to see you again! Well, hear you anyway. Remember when you said you'd be there to help us some time when we REALLY needed it?" He listened again and smiled. "Yup. I know the cage can only be opened with a code." Karl frowned. "You don't have it? Darn. Okay, I have another idea. How much can you lift?"

HE LISTENED FOR ANOTHER SECOND, THEN BEAMED. "Excellent!" Then he whispered into the cone and sat back against the bars. He crossed his arms with a satisfied smile. "**NOW WE WAIT.**"

"For?"

Karl wagged his finger. "Shhh. Patience."

"**TELL THAT TO THE MISSILES!!!!**" DJ said.

But Karl smiled wider and began whistling the theme to *Hockey Night in Canada*.

Ten minutes later, he pointed to a blinking red dot moving quickly along the floor of the tunnel toward them.

"Is that a mind-control wristwatch?" Starlight asked.

"Petunia's." Karl reached between the bars and grabbed it. "Splort, you rock!"

He **WRAPPED THE WATCH AROUND THE BARS**. "Like I said, Fuzzy **TOLD US EVERYTHING** we needed to know."

"Such as?" asked the twins.

"One: We knew **PETUNIA WAS DROPPING THIS IN THE TRUCK**. Two: Fuzzy taught us that **SIZE CAN WORK AGAINST YOU**. We're trapped in here, not because of the bars, but because we can't fit between them."

"But an Ice Squid can," Starlight said. "How did you know Splort would be here?"

"I took **A CALCULATED CHANCE**. Splort had told us to just call her if we needed help. Fuzzy told us this was the cage from **RINK 53**, so I figured there was a shot **AT LEAST ONE OF THE SQUIDS MIGHT HAVE JUMPED IN WHEN FUZZY TOOK THE CAGE**."

"They are naturally curious," DJ said. "And love to travel."

"Yes. And Fuzzy didn't know that the rink thaws out between our practices. I refreeze it fresh each time to save electricity. So the Squids hang out in the colder parts of the rink."

"Like this cage," Starlight said. "IMPRESSIVE REASONING, CAPTAIN."

He gave Starlight a nudge on the shoulder. "You must be rubbing off on me."

Starlight shook her head, smiling. "And you also used Fuzzy's own aggression, his desire to get us whacked by a missile, against him."

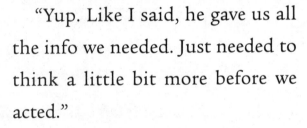

"Yup. Like I said, he gave us all the info we needed. Just needed to think a little bit more before we acted."

"A team isn't just the two of us, or even the six of us. It's **ALL** the people we rely on," said the twins.

"Including Ice Squids!" Starlight smiled.

DJ scratched the top of his helmet. "Okay, but what is the plan exactly?"

Karl smiled. "Splort, take cover." He waited a minute until he was sure the microscopic Squid had found a safe place to hide. "DJ, I need your, frankly frightening, stick skills for a second. Pretend this wristband is skating through your crease."

DJ SMILED AND HELD HIS STICK UP IN THE AIR, POISED OVER THE BARS.

"Good. Benny and Jenny, get ready to squirt all the water in your bottles into the air in front of us."

"**ON IT,**" said the twins.

"How about me?" asked Mo.

"You'll be a key component in just a second," Karl said. He turned to Starlight. "How much time do you estimate I'll have?"

Starlight ran back all the times she'd seen these wristbands self-destruct. "3.242 seconds from impact."

"Good. Okay. DJ whacks the watch to break it. Then—"

But DJ, thinking that was his cue, whacked the watch.

"**YIKES!**" Karl yelled.

"**SQUIRT! NOW!**" said Starlight.

The twins squirted and Karl froze a solid wall of ice in front of the team **JUST AS THE WATCH EXPLODED**.

The force threw the Six against the back of the cell, surrounded by shards of shattered ice. But they were unharmed.

Mo coughed away the smoke and mist. "**THE BARS ARE STILL THERE!**" he said. "It didn't work!"

Karl put a hand on his shoulder. "*Au contraire, mon ami*. This is where you come in — using your strength for good." Karl pointed at the bars, which were **GLOWING WHITE HOT**.

Mo cracked his knuckles and marched over. He grabbed the bars, stretching them apart, straining under the effort and the sting of the hot metal on his gloved hands. But when he stepped back there was a gap big enough for even Mo to go through.

Karl blew cold air onto the bars and then jumped through.

"Splort, you coming?" Karl called. He flash-froze his water bottle and tipped it down to the ground.

The others jumped through the gap and they made their way down the tunnel toward Ron and the waiting copter.

"Where to now?" asked the twins.

Karl pointed up. "Didn't Petunia say something about hot springs?"

Starlight gave Karl a high-five. "Great job, captain. One question: Why didn't you just give Splort your comm link and have her take it up top to call Ron for help?"

"Um." Karl's face fell slightly. "I guess we could do that next time."

CHAPTER TWENTY-TWO
THE RAB–BIT OFF MORE THAN HE COULD CHEW

Fuzzy and Petunia looked into the distance at the blue sky above snow-peaked mountains. It was nearing sunset.

"They're late for a very important date," Fuzzy said with a scowl. The **SIZEMATRON 2000 STRAPPED TO HIS BACK** shifted, and he checked to make sure the switch was still set to **"BIGGIFY."** It was.

Petunia put an ear to the ground. "Yes, they should be here."

"Here" was Banff National Park, home to skiing, golf, mountains and hot springs. And Fuzzy and Petunia were about to reroute the Bow River to wash out the entire valley.

All it would take was about 100 super rabbits digging furiously to collapse the side of Mount Norquay and, as Fuzzy put it, *whoosh* — another human degradation of nature would disappear.

He had it all mapped out. **FIRST, BLAST BANFF**. From there it would be on to . . . **NIAGARA FALLS**: "We get some beavers to help us dam the river, and Lake Erie will back up and take care of Cleveland, Buffalo and most of the towns on the river."

YELLOWSTONE PARK: "That giant volcano underneath just needs a little nudge and it's goodbye to the Midwest."

The **CHURCHILL FALLS POWER PLANT** in Newfoundland: "The whole island might just drift away like an iceberg."

And so on and so on . . .

Of course, some of you may live in or near these places. So unless you're covered in lava, or floating on top of an iceberg in the Atlantic, or under hundreds of metres of unexpected water . . . you know this did not happen.

What saved the continent from certain furry destruction? **DOES THIS HOCKEY JERSEY ANSWER YOUR QUESTION?**

YES!

Say it with me: **THE HOCKEY SUPER SIX!**

But how? Back to the bunnies . . .

"What's taking the kids so long?" Petunia seemed worried. That's because she was worried. She put her ears to the ground listening for the patter of hundreds of furry feet digging underground.

SUDDENLY THE TREETOPS BEGAN TO SWAY.

"That's odd," Petunia said. **"There was no wind in the forecast."**

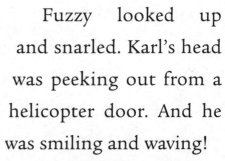

Fuzzy looked up and snarled. Karl's head was peeking out from a helicopter door. And he was smiling and waving!

"HEY THERE, FUZZY!" Karl yelled. "How's the wanton destruction going?"

"HOW DID YOU ESCAPE?" Fuzzy yelled. "You were trapped! **MISSILES WERE ON THE WAY!"**

"WELL, NEVER UNDERESTIMATE THE VALUE OF FRIENDS," Karl smiled. The other five popped their heads out next to his.

"And the missiles?"

Karl snorted. **"THERE WERE NEVER ANY MISSILES COMING."**

"HA! You're lying! I heard your mother say they were intercepting my children."

"I thought **YOU MIGHT BE LISTENING IN,** with those ears of yours. But I know my mom, and she is not the type to blow up a bunch of mind-controlled bunnies just because they stole some gold."

Petunia shook her fist at Karl. **"Then where are my children?"**

"Funny bunny story. I had to bite my lip to

stop from laughing when Fuzzy here joked about **DRONES WITH BUNNY-CATCHING NETS.**"

"Wha—?"

There was a sudden whoosh of wind as **AN ARMY OF DRONES** poured over the top of the nearby hotel. **EACH CARRIED A SMALL FURRY BUNNY IN A STEEL NET.**

"Mom! Dad!" cried the chorus of captured rabbits.

"MY BABIES!" Petunia hollered.

"One of DJ's ideas, actually," Karl said.

DJ waved his webbed goalie glove. **"GOALIES ALWAYS KNOW THE BEST WAY TO CATCH THINGS."**

Fuzzy let out a howl.

The side window of the copter slid open and PM PP appeared. "How about we discuss this over a nice dinner of lettuce and radishes?"

"YOU'LL HAVE TO CAPTURE US FIRST," Fuzzy yelled. "Come, Petunia. We can dig our way out of here."

Petunia stood rooted to the spot, staring up at her captured kittens*. "Fuzzy, we can't just leave them. What if they drop them into the hot springs? They'll be instant *hassenpfeffer*!" She gasped. "I've got to save them!"

Petunia leaped up to grab for her nearest kid, but the drone backed just far enough away. She fell back to earth, dejected.

"Try again," Starlight muttered quietly. "Just a little higher."

----

*YES! The actual name for baby rabbits! MORE KNOWLEDGE!

Petunia leaped again, this time even higher.

"FIRE!" Starlight yelled.

Ron pushed a button, and a drone, hidden behind the copter, shot out and sprung its net at Petunia. "I'm caught!" she yelled as **THE STEEL NET CLOSED AROUND HER**. The drone, built for tiny rabbits, struggled to stay aloft.

"Now fly away!" PM PP called out. The drones with the children sped into the distance, but Petunia's lagged behind.

"Fuzzy," Petunia called. "DO SOMETHING."

But what could Fuzzy do? His mind raced. Escape? And leave behind his family? Attack and possibly put them all at risk? Chase after them and think of a new plan on the way?

WHAT COULD **ONE REGULAR-SIZED** BUNNY EVEN DO?

Regular sized!

He remembered the weapon strapped to his back.

PM PP called down. "Fuzzy, give up now and I'm sure we can come to a peaceful arrangement."

"I'VE GOT BIGGER PLANS!" Fuzzy yelled. He quickly swung the gun around to point at himself, then shot. Fuzzy howled as his body was bathed in electric blue light. **HE GREW BIGGER AND BIGGERER AND EVEN BIGGERERER.**

"HAHAHAHAHAHAHA!!!!" he laughed. **BUT HIS FINGER GOT CAUGHT IN THE TRIGGER** and he continued to expand, like a balloon. "NO!!!"

"HE'S GOING TO BLOW UP!" yelled the twins.

DJ leaped from the copter without waiting for more instructions. He flew straight at the weapon, and in one quick slash of his stick, shattered the trigger guard. He hit the ground hard and rolled away.

The gun landed in a pile of pine needles next to DJ's motionless body.

Fuzzy stood up. He **NOW TOWERED OVER THE TALLEST TREES**. He stared down at DJ, who shook his head as he recovered from his fall. Fuzzy **GRABBED A NEARBY TREE** and snapped the trunk clean off. Then he bent the trunk into the shape of **A GIANT HOCKEY STICK**.

DJ got his bearings and looked at the bunny. "You okay there, Fuzzy?"

"Never better," Fuzzy said. He quickly swung the tree back and then forward. A **PERFECT SLAP SHOT SENT DJ HURTLING THROUGH THE AIR** toward the distant river.

"DJ!!!!" yelled his teammates. The twins slid down Fuzzy's back and sped toward the river.

Fuzzy ignored them and turned his attention to Petunia. But she was now out of reach, high in the sky trailing after the kits. But the copter was still dangerously close.

"You'll pay for this!" he yelled.

"Gulp," said PM PP, sliding her window shut.

Fuzzy reached out and snagged the copter's tail. The engine squealed as **RON TRIED, IN VAIN, TO ESCAPE THE GIANT'S GRIP**. Fuzzy bit off the rotors and pulled the copter right up to his giant pink nose. **HIS RED EYES FLASHED**.

"Now, you pathetic humans," his voice shook the trees and echoed off the mountains, "it's time for Fuzzy to finish what he started."

CHAPTER TWENTY-THREE
FURRY-IOUS FINISH

Fuzzy didn't release his grip on the copter as he **MARCHED IN PURSUIT OF THE DRONES**. His footsteps pounded the ground, bouncing boulders into the air like pebbles. He could see Petunia and the children as dots in the distance. In **JUST A FEW MORE STEPS** he'd be there.

But then he stopped. **"WAIT."** He chuckled and shook his head. He lifted the copter up to his face again. "No. That's exactly what you want me to do."

The drones hovered just above the roofline as if they were waiting for Fuzzy to follow.

Fuzzy crunched down on the copter roof. Inside, the PM, Ron, Starlight, Karl and Mo huddled together. The metal squealed as it closed in on their heads. Mo struggled to stop the metal from collapsing.

"NICE TRY," Fuzzy bellowed. "Using my own **FAMILY AS BAIT**. What's behind the hotel? An army with a giant net and cables?"

PM PP smacked her forehead. **FILBERT AND THE**

ARMY WERE INDEED HIDING THERE WITH A GIANT NET AND CABLES.

"I'm not sure you were prepared for a bunny this big, but I don't plan to find out. **CALL BACK THOSE DRONES OR I WILL CRUSH YOU LIKE A CAN OF TOMATOES.**"

"Shoot," said PM PP. She spoke into her comm link. "Filbert, he's on to us."

"Shhh," Starlight said. She pointed at her own ears, as a warning that Fuzzy could, of course, hear everything they said.

PM PP turned off her comm link and mouthed. "Now what?"

Starlight tapped Mo's knee.

Here's one of the bits of info you need to know about these kids' school: The GOOBERS curriculum includes numerous language classes, and Mo and Starlight had both taken **AMERICAN SIGN LANGUAGE**.

Mo looked at Starlight and nodded. **HE SIGNED "PLANS?"** Starlight nodded and signed back, **"SIZEMATRON 2000."** They continued back and forth, including "bunny," "hope" and "help."

"I don't hear any talking and I haven't crushed you YET," Fuzzy bellowed. **"ARE YOU DEAD?"**

"Put us down and I'll call back the drones," yelled the PM.

"Call back the drones first," said Fuzzy.

PM PP stared out the cracked front window and caught a glimpse of dust rising in the distance.

Ron activated his telescopic vision. **"IT'S THE**

TWINS, WITH DJ!" he signed.

Starlight saw a possible solution in an instant. But would there be enough time?

"DO IT NOW!" Fuzzy yelled, crushing down harder on the copter's hull.

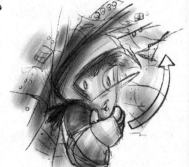

Starlight signed the word "scream."

"AHHHHHH!!!!!!!!!!" yelled everyone in the copter.

Using the noise as cover, Patinage whispered "fly" into her comm link. And instead of flying toward Fuzzy, the drones, with his children and Petunia, sped away and up over the mountains.

"FUZZY!" Petunia yelled. Fuzzy swung his head and **HOWLED AS HIS FAMILY TURNED INTO TINY SPECKS IN THE DISTANCE.**

Were they safe? Were they in danger?

Fuzzy (smart bunny) refused to jump to conclusions.

BUT he was furious. Petunia and his children were gone. His plans were crumbling faster than a poorly dug tunnel. "REVENGE!"

HE CRUSHED THE COPTER.

Luckily for the rest of this book, Starlight had used the momentary distraction to **SIGN "JUMP."** Karl had quickly frozen a slide that slowed their fall, and Mo had crushed it into splinters before Fuzzy could turn back around.

Fuzzy sensed something was wrong when the debris in **HIS HAND FAILED TO YIELD MORE SCREAMS OR THE CRUNCHING OF BONES**. He looked down at the forest floor where the Six and the others were scrambling for cover.

"I WILL CRUSH YOU ALL!" Fuzzy said. He threw the debris of the copter at PM PP, but Mo was able to hip check the wreckage away at the last moment. "I'll squash you like the bugs you are!" Fuzzy stomped angrily and frantically.

"So aggressive," Starlight said. "Okay, let's see if we've thought this through."

Patinage saw Starlight give her a nod. **"KARL! NOW!"** she yelled.

Karl **FROZE THE GROUND**, and Banff became a super-sized rink.

Starlight spoke into her comm link. "Find that weapon!"

Super hockey players now darted at top speed around the trees beneath Fuzzy. They were looking for the **SIZEMATRON 2000**, and trying to avoid Fuzzy's feet . . . with mixed results.

"**IT'S NOT HERE!**" Karl yelled, zipping around tree after tree.

Fuzzy's foot slammed down again and again. He caught Mo, **HAMMERING HIM LIKE A NAIL** two metres into the ground.

Mo struggled to loosen the ice and dirt.

Fuzzy turned his attention to Starlight and succeeded in catching the edge of her sledge with his big toe. She flew through the air and landed in the boughs of an enormous Douglas fir.

The twins arrived at that moment, carrying a soaking wet DJ on their shoulders. **AND DJ WAS CARRYING THE SIZEMATRON 2000!** He aimed it at Fuzzy.

"I told you goalies know how to grab things," DJ yelled. "I snatched it just before you whacked me into the river. And now, **GET READY TO SHRINK**."

HE PULLED THE TRIGGER.

CHAPTER TWENTY-FOUR
PUN-INTENDED
CONEY-SEQUENCES

One last LAST bit of brain food before we see what happens next. Often our actions have what are known as **"UNINTENDED CONSEQUENCES, "** and they can be pretty bad. These are things we didn't think of before we acted — things we didn't even consider might happen.

So, for example, everything seemed great about what DJ was doing. He had grabbed the **SIZEMATRON 2000**. He had aimed it at Fuzzy. And he planned to shrink him back down to bunny-sized so they could catch him.

You remember that this had happened before, with the unintended consequence that Fuzzy had escaped? But, DJ figured, this time they knew he'd try that, so he told Karl to get ready to freeze the bunny in a block of ice.

This resulted in Karl being right next to Fuzzy when DJ fired. BUT DJ didn't factor in that (a) when he'd slashed the weapon's handle he'd inadvertently **BROKEN THE REVERSE SWITCH** and (b) that **A BIG BUNNY IS STILL A FAST BUNNY**.

So he fired. The switch, even though set to "reverse," was still actually stuck on "biggify."

Fuzzy had heard the weapon warming up, and he kicked Karl into the path of the beam just as DJ pulled the trigger. **THE ENERGY BEAM HIT KARL.**

"HA HA!" bellowed Fuzzy. "A tiny Karl will be so easy to stomp!"

But, there was one more **UNINTENDED CONSEQUENCE**, which is that **A GIANT BUNNY IS NO MATCH FOR A GIANT ICE SQUID.**

YES, the beam didn't actually hit Karl — it hit his water bottle. Splort burst from Karl's belt, growing bigger and bigger.

"NOOOO!!!!!" yelled Fuzzy. He threw a tree, which whacked Splort right in the eye. This had the **UNINTENDED CONSEQUENCE** of making Splort even angrier. Splort came at Fuzzy with all eight arms **WHIPPING LIKE DEMENTED SNAKES.**

What followed was an epic battle for the ages.

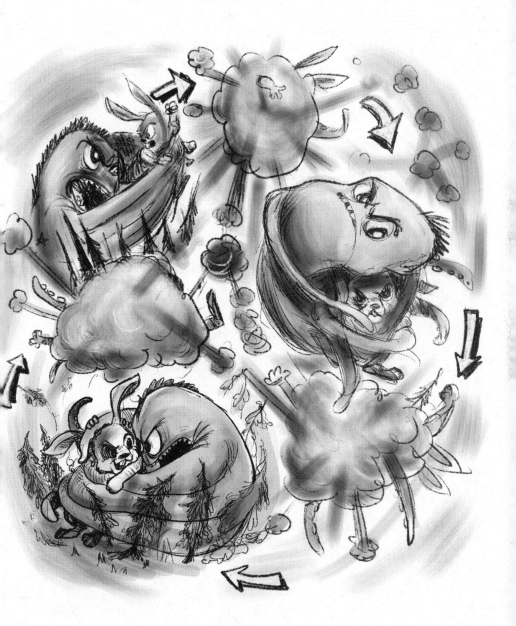

The dust settled. The Super Six and friends dared to skate closer to see the final result. A breeze rose, lifting away the cloud, and the Super Six cheered as they saw Splort had wrapped Fuzzy in the **UNBREAKABLE GRIP** of a giant Ice Squid.

Except, you guessed it, this had the **UNINTENDED CONSEQUENCE** of making Splort, fueled by **SIZEMATRON 2000-INDUCED RAGE**, notice them. Her tentacles began to slacken.

"Oops," said Mo, his head sticking out from the ground. "Not again."

Starlight turned on DJ, "QUICK! Give it to me." He handed her the weapon. Starlight pulled a screwdriver out of a secret pocket and quickly began tinkering with the dial. Karl and DJ began digging Mo out of the ground.

"HURRY!" said everyone about everything.

Fuzzy was almost free. Splort gnashed her teeth at the kids. **STARLIGHT FIRED.**

Blue energy formed a halo around both beasts and **THEY SHRANK, AND SHRANK SOME MORE.** Starlight was careful to shrink them at the same rate so that Fuzzy couldn't escape Splort's grasp.

Finally, they had shrunk down to an ordinary-sized rabbit being held by a bigger-than-ordinary Ice Squid.

"SORRY ABOUT THE ALMOST EATING YOU THING," Splort said. "Can you make me microscopic again?"

"In just a second,"

Starlight said, patting her on the head. "And thanks AGAIN." Splort smiled, even as Fuzzy tried to wriggle free.

Filbert, driving an enormous armoured truck, appeared from behind the hotel. More trucks followed. Robots with titanium cables appeared from their cabs and sped toward the bunny, **GATHERING HIM IN TIGHT NETTING**. He howled and kicked, and bit . . . but he was finally, and completely, **CAPTURED**.

"REVENGE!" Fuzzy yelled. "I'll get you all!"

"**SO AGGRESSIVE,**" Starlight said. She shook one of Splort's tentacles and then blasted her with the ray. Splort waved as she shrank.

"**UNTIL NEXT TIME,**" she said. Just as she disappeared into the ice, the **SIZEMATRON 2000** sputtered and broke apart.

"Good riddance," said Mo.

DJ SMASHED IT INTO EVEN MORE PIECES WITH HIS STICK. He looked at the twins, and pointed at his eyes with two fingers, then at the twins' eyes. "Stay out of my crease."

"You got it!" they said.

Patinage walked over to Fuzzy and knelt down. "I am sorry for everything, Fuzzy. I meant it when I said I wanted a peaceful solution for all of us."

"You lie! My children. Petunia!!!!!" The rabbit's **EYES DARTED AROUND** looking for signs of his family.

Patinage snapped her fingers and the robots lifted Fuzzy, kicking and screaming, to the back of the largest truck.

"I think this will make you happy," she said.

The doors to the truck swung open wide. The back of the truck was **FILLED WITH A HUNDRED AND ONE BUNNIES**. They were all happily munching on carrots and lettuce and chatting away behind a floor-to-ceiling Plexiglas screen.

Petunia, seeing Fuzzy, pushed herself against the divider, reaching out to hug him. Fuzzy stopped struggling. He stared lovingly at Petunia. Tears formed in his eyes.

Patinage sighed. "We never intended any harm. And there's more good news, hopefully for everyone." Filbert appeared at her side, along with Karl and a woman in a lab coat. "This is Dr. Kinnian."

"Mr. Fuzzywinkle. We at GUMPP Laboratories have developed a way to reverse the effects of Crosscheck's mind control wristbands without taking away any of the benefits."

Fuzzy narrowed his eyes. "How?"

"Karl," she said. "With some observations from Starlight."

Karl pointed at his head. "I wasn't affected the same way by Crosscheck's band. So they found something in here," he tapped his helmet, "that works like a kind of **IMMUNITY VACCINE**."

"I find it highly unlikely they found anything in there," DJ joked.

Even Karl had to chuckle at that.

Dr. Killian held up a syringe filled with an ice blue liquid, with some kind of crystals floating inside. "If you are interested, we can give you the treatment right now."

Petunia was nodding. She pointed behind her at the happy children, and then at her own arm. She had a bandage with a smiley face.

Fuzzy struggled. Were they lying? But one more look into Petunia's eyes showed that she was not. A horrible voice in his head yelled "NO!" **BUT HE FOUGHT IT AND NODDED.** "Fine."

Dr. Kinnian gave him the shot. His body relaxed and he stopped struggling. His eyes began to soften.

"I see," he said. "Crosscheck. His thoughts and words were **IN MY HEAD.**"

Starlight came up next to him. "I had surmised, observing the way **KARL HAD REPEATED CROSSCHECK'S ORDERS WORD FOR WORD**, and the **IRRATIONAL ANGER** of the squids, the geckos and your family, that part of the wavelengths programmed into the bands were **DIRECT EVIL THOUGHTS FROM HIS VERY MIND**."

Dr. Kinnian put a bandage on Fuzzy's arm. "Kind of like a horrible computer virus."

"And it's gone now?" Fuzzy listened for any trace of the voice. *Was it gone?*

Patinage watched him carefully, then signalled for the robots to release Fuzzy.

"We're sorry for what happened to you," Patinage said. "Sorry for what Crosscheck did and for what we humans have been doing. We promise to do better."

"I'd like to join my family now."

Patinage nodded. Stairs appeared from the back of the truck, and the Plexiglas shield rolled up into the ceiling of the van. The Super Six flinched, but **NO ONE TRIED TO ESCAPE**. Instead the bunnies surrounded Fuzzy like a giant mob of happy, playful stuffed toys.

The van doors closed and peace reigned in the valley.

Mo climbed out of the hole and clapped the dirt off his jersey. Then he spoke the magic word: **"PIZZA?"**

CHAPTER TWENTY-FIVE
THE END OF A FUZZY TAIL

Ron pushed a button on his rear end and a film began showing on the wall of Pauline Patinage's office. A **DRONE FLEW LOW OVER ROLLING OCEAN WAVES** on a clear blue sky, and then descended toward an emerald green island. **BUNNIES HOPPED HAPPILY ABOUT**, some of them building lean-to homes, some making pottery, and others harvesting delicious-looking carrots, rutabagas, radishes and lettuce.

"This is McGregor Island," the PM said. "One

of the islands off the coast of BC. A perfect haven for our bunnies."

The drone flew lower and bunnies waved. The drone zoomed in on a **CONTENTED-LOOKING FUZZY SITTING ON A LAWN CHAIR**, sporting sunglasses and sipping a drink from a coconut with an umbrella sticking out. Petunia was sitting next to him, reading a book about a kid chef who was also a detective.

"They seem happy," Starlight said.

Karl popped a pepperoni in his mouth. "What more can you ask for? Good food. Good books. Good friends."

Mo leaned over. "You talking about the bunnies, or us?"

Karl just smiled.

"So the antidote worked," said the twins. **"HURRAY FOR SCIENCE!"**

DJ wasn't quite as enthusiastic. "Bunnies have a **NATURAL MEAN STREAK**. Sure, making him bigger made him meaner. But you guys keep forgetting **HE WAS PRETTY MEAN WHEN HE WAS SMALL**."

The screen was filled with waving bunnies, smiling and dancing. Then the drone zoomed back out and the movie ended. Ron pressed his butt and projection stopped.

Pauline Patinage clapped her hands and the lights came back up. "Perhaps DJ is right. Which is why, as a precaution, McGregor Island is remote."

Starlight began counting on her fingers. "One: It's an island so, ergo, no connection back to the mainland. And *Oryctolagus cuniculus* aren't big swimmers. Two: The water off the coast of B.C. doesn't freeze in winter. Three: There are no trees, so it's easy for the GUMPP satellites to see everything that moves. Right?"

"And GUMPP has probably made sure it doesn't show up on any maps," DJ said.

Patinage blushed. "I promised Fuzzy that we would do everything to make sure he and his family were happy and safe. But I also have a duty to keep everyone else safe as well."

Karl raised a glass of root beer. "**TO ANOTHER MISSION WELL DONE!**"

They all clinked glasses and then went back to chatting and eating pizza. The world was safe again.

WHAT COULD POSSIBLY BE WORSE THAN AN EVIL RABBIT?

EPILOGUE
FUREVER HOME

Fuzzy watched the latest GUMPP drone peel away and disappear into the low clouds. He put down his drink and stood up. The waves lapped on the rocky shore, dappled in sunlight. His children happily played and frolicked on the green fields behind him.

"Isn't it wonderful here?" Petunia said, taking his arm in hers.

"PARADISE," Fuzzy said with a smile.

She kissed him on the cheek. "I'll go see what

the kids have planned for dinner. See you back at the warren soon?"

Fuzzy nodded and went back to staring at the horizon. In the far distance he could see the shoreline of the mainland like a thin strip of green on the horizon. He cocked his ears and heard a distant bell, a buoy in the middle of the water. By the echo he estimated that it was about a half a league away. **HE NARROWED HIS EYES** and could see a green light blinking on and off. Yes, this was paradise, **BUT WASN'T IT ALSO A PRISON?** Too far to swim. Too deep to dig.

The water was blue and beautiful. But hadn't the cold blue steel of his basement cage been beautiful in its own way? Could he even consider if there was a better . . .

"DINNER!" Petunia called from their home in the side of a hill.

"Coming!" Fuzzy turned and shook his head, trying to shake away the silly thoughts.

AND YET.

He stared at the water again. The  wind sent a spray of mist toward him. He held up his paw and marvelled again as just the lightest touch turned the mist into delicate snowflakes.

Maybe there was a way? His brilliant mind began to think. But then, just as he was about to think an incredible thought, he was thrown to the ground . . . by the **BIGGEST EARTHQUAKE IN THE HISTORY OF THE WORLD . . .**

ACKNOWLEDGEMENTS

So this is the third book in this series. If you enjoyed it, that's only partly thanks to me. BIG-TIME assists go to Anne Shone and Yvonne Lam. They made working through a pandemic seem . . . almost like a regular season hockey game, instead of the dangerous matches the Six are getting used to playing. Also my family, who support me so much it makes me bawl like a baby sometimes. And I'm a Buffalo Sabres fan, so I cry a lot.

And can I just say that when I make fun of scientists in these books, it's not to throw even the slightest shade at ACTUAL scientists or science. THANKS to all the scientists who helped develop the vaccines! Thanks to science for making my life better almost every day. And thanks to you, who looked for some silliness to help you get through a rough time. You've helped keep me and this series going.

All this is to say: it takes a team to make a book. And teamwork is what these books are all about. The Six didn't start out as pals; they have grown to appreciate each other.

Sometimes we get "teamwork" wrong. We think it means working with people we agree with, in a happy, happy, hugs-and-smiles world. No. I've played hockey my whole life and have not agreed with everyone I've played with — about hockey and about other things. Teamwork means finding a way to work together toward a common goal, despite those differences. That goal could be well, a goal. Or it could be making the world a better, more welcoming place. But whatever it is, it's finding a way to work with people you don't see eye to eye with all the time.

Is it easy? Of course not! Hockey isn't easy either. But it can be fun. It's how you decide to play it that makes the difference.

HOCKEY SUPER SIX